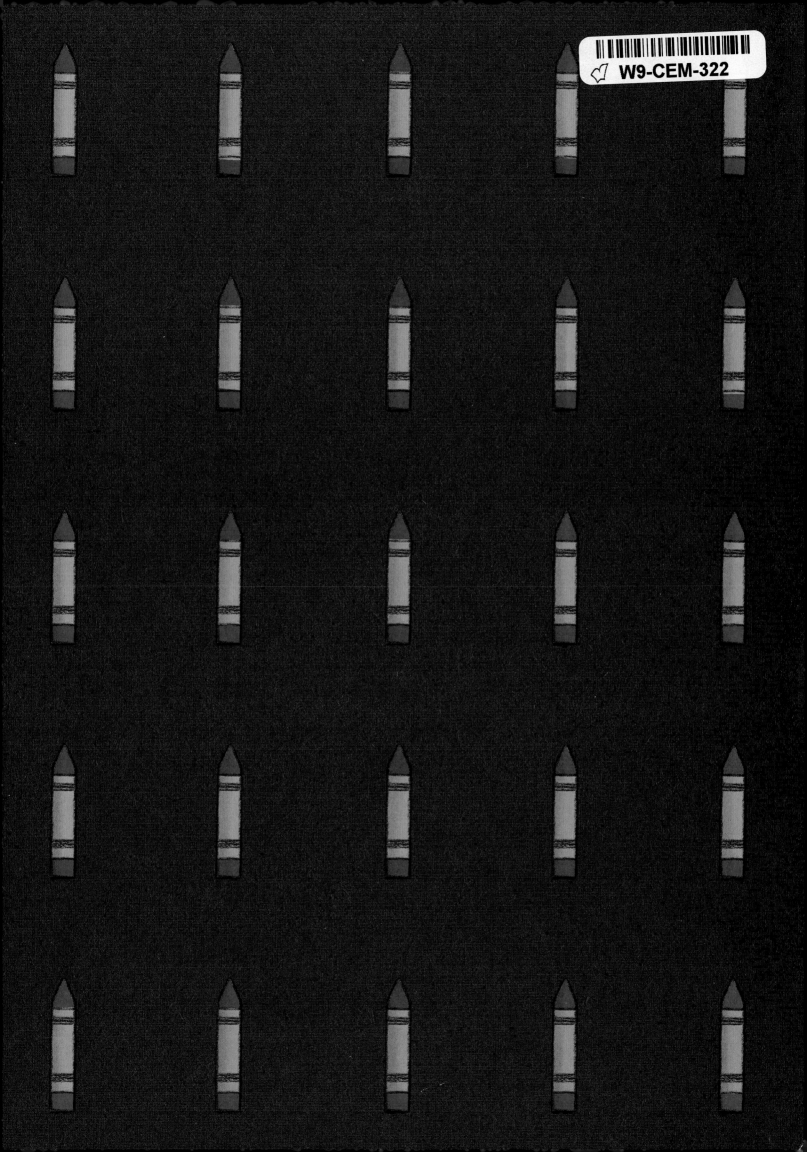

W9-CEM-322

CRE

CRA

WORDS
AARON REYNOLDS

PICTURES
PETER BROWN

SIMON & SCHUSTER BOOKS FOR YOUNG READERS
New York   London   Toronto   Sydney   New Delhi

Jasper Rabbit was struggling in school.
He was flunking math. He was failing spelling.
The only subject he was passing was art.
Jasper needed serious help.

That's when he found . . . the crayon.

It was purple.
Pointy.
And perfect.

And somehow . . .
it looked happy to see him.

That night, Jasper knew he had to study for his spelling test. But TALES FROM THE CARROT PATCH was on! By the time it was over, he was way too tired to study.

The test was a disaster.

Jasper couldn't
remember how to
spell a single word.

That's when he noticed
something strange.

Jasper picked up the crayon.

Immediately, he spelled all
the words correctly!

Jasper Spelling
2-L

Ocean
Yellow
Courage

When he got his test back, he got
an A-plus and a sticker!
The crayon looked . . . pleased.

Creepy.
But cool.

After dinner, Jasper settled in to play BUNNY BRAWL 3.

"Math homework first," said Dad.
"Fine," moaned Jasper.

That's when he saw it. Scrawled in peculiar purple penmanship.

WHO NEEDS MATH WHEN YOU HAVE BUNNY BRAWL 3?

SPELLING
MATH

Three hours later he fell asleep.
His game in one hand.
The purple crayon in the other.

When Mrs. Lopshire announced a surprise math quiz, Jasper panicked! He reached for a pencil. But instead his hand wrapped around the crayon.

Suddenly, math seemed easy! He knew when to carry the one. He knew when to borrow from the bigger numbers. It was like the crayon knew exactly what to do.

After the quiz, he saw it.
Written on his backpack.

JASPER
+
CRAYON
4EVER

Jasper felt a shiver
go up his spine.

The next day was the deadline for the poster contest. Jasper had been working on his entry for weeks. It just needed a few finishing touches.

The purple crayon rolled across the table.

All by itself.

But Jasper ignored it.

He shuddered. He scrubbed the writing off the table. He zipped the crayon into his pencil case.

He tried to forget all about the crayon.

But when he woke up, his precious artwork . . . was better than ever!

It was a horrifying masterpiece . . . in PURPLE!!!

"Fantastic work!" cried Mr. Hoppypott.
"You should be very proud!"
But Jasper didn't feel proud.
He felt eeked out.
Freaked out.
Creeped out!

When he got home, Jasper
descended into the deepest,
darkest corner of his basement.

He put the crayon
in a dusty box.

And locked it tight.

He went to bed feeling much better.

But when he woke up the next day . . .
THERE! On the mirror!

In his pencil case . . . the creepy crayon!

And it looked happy to see him.

That day, Jasper got all A-pluses.

It was terrible.

Enough was enough!
Jasper snapped the creepy crayon in two.

He melted it in the microwave.

And he threw the mess
into the garbage.

He drifted to sleep that night, feeling relieved.

But when he woke up . . .
THERE! On his wall!
It was a mural of him graduating
elementary school. With straight
As. And worst of all . . . it was
really well drawn.

STRAIGHT
As!!!

And next to it . . .
THE CREEPY CRAYON!

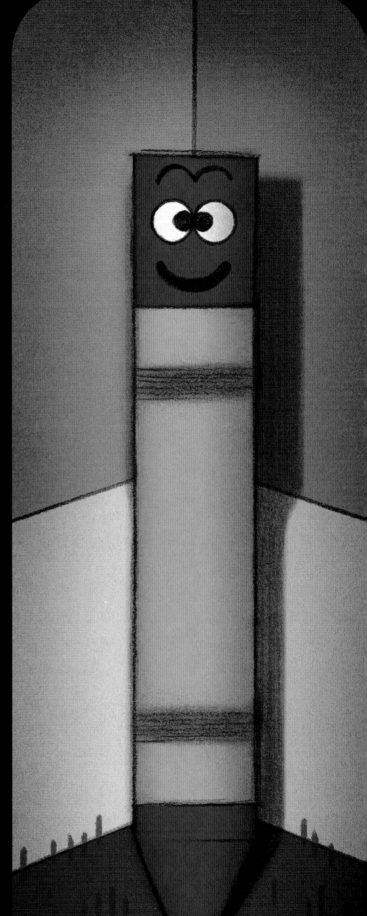

Purple. Pointy. And perfect.

All day, no matter what Jasper did, the creepy crayon was there. Looking oh-so-pleased.

IN HIS HAND!
As he aced his vocabulary quiz.

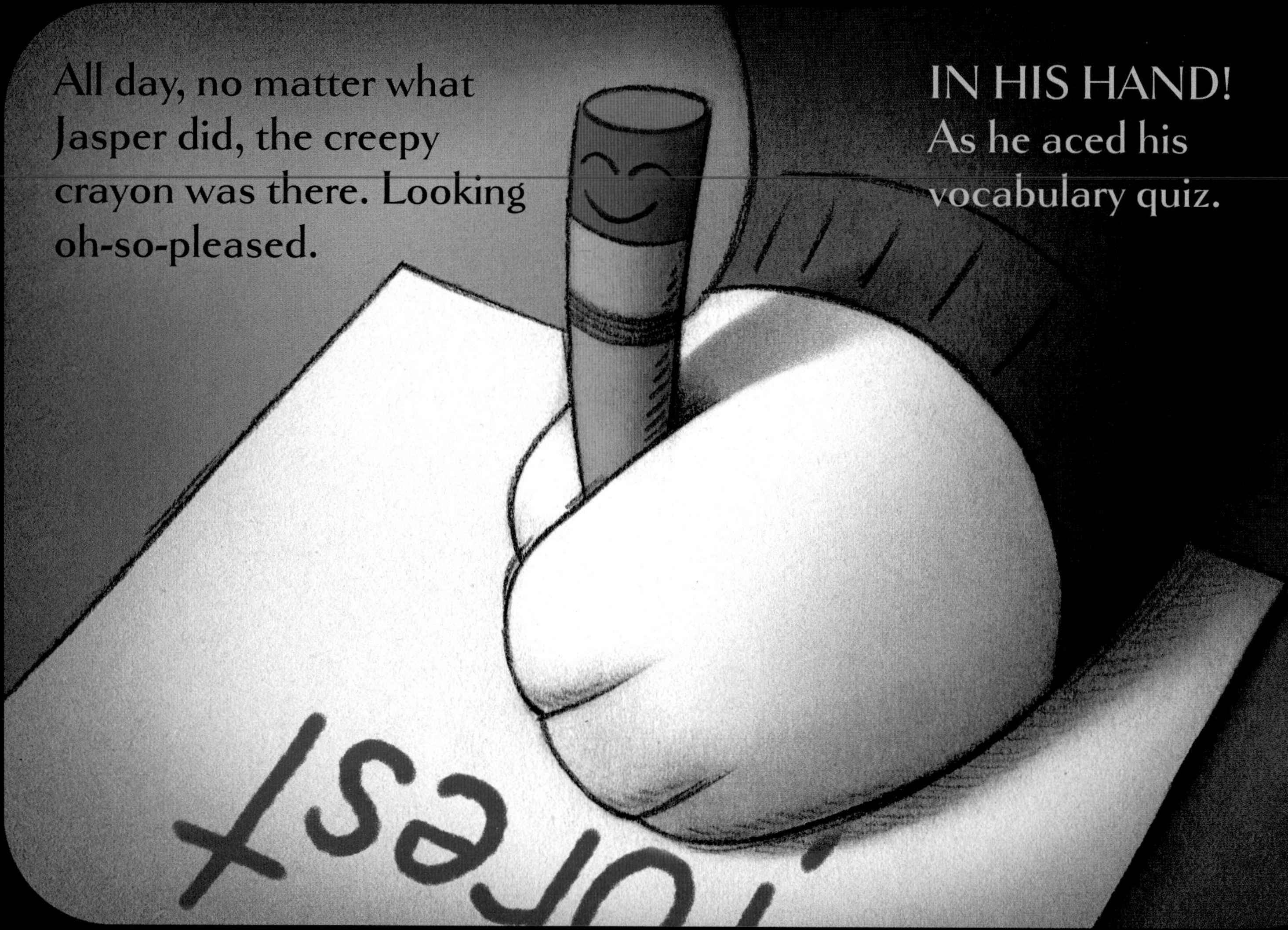

IN HIS POCKET!
As Mrs. Lopshire named Jasper MOST IMPROVED STUDENT.

IN THE CROWD! As the school celebrated Jasper in a special assembly.

Things were spinning out of control!

Jasper couldn't take it anymore. When he got home, he ran straight to the toilet.

And he threw the crayon in. It just floated there, spinning slowly. It did not look happy to see him.

And then Jasper saw it. Scribbled inside the bowl.

DON'T. YOU. DARE.

But Jasper dared.

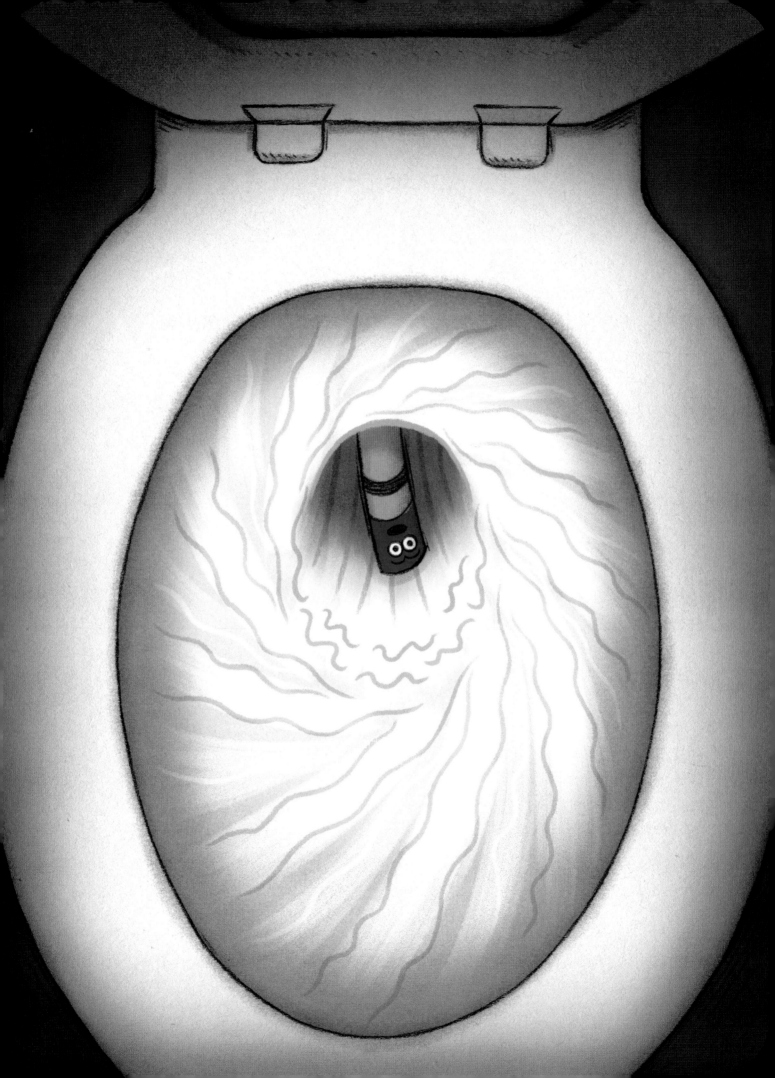

That evening, TALES FROM THE
CARROT PATCH was on. But Jasper . . .
studied for his spelling test.

His eyes kept darting to his pencil case.
No creepy crayon.

He flung the toilet lid up.
No creepy crayon.

He got into bed, nervously
watching his walls.
No. Creepy. Crayon.

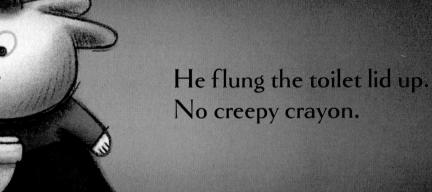

During the test, Jasper spelled OCEAN wrong.
But he spelled COURAGE right!

He got a C-plus.
It was glorious.
It wasn't an A.
But it was his.

He headed home from school
that day, finally feeling free.

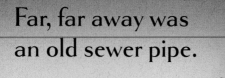

Far, far away was
an old sewer pipe.

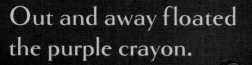

Out and away floated
the purple crayon.

Slowly . . . silently . . . it drifted.
For days. And weeks.

One thing was clear.
The creepy crayon would never
cause trouble ever again.

Except . . . that's when Elliot Pelican
spotted the creepy crayon.

It was purple.
Pointy.
And perfect.

And somehow . . .
it looked happy to see him.

To Rod Serling, Vincent Price, and Roald Dahl . . .
the masters of creepy AND funny —A. R.

To Dr. O'Boyle, art teacher extraordinaire —P. B.

SIMON & SCHUSTER BOOKS FOR YOUNG READERS
An imprint of Simon & Schuster Children's Publishing Division
1230 Avenue of the Americas, New York, New York 10020
Text © 2022 by Aaron Reynolds
Illustration © 2022 by Peter Brown
Book design by Lizzy Bromley © 2022 by Simon & Schuster, Inc.
All rights reserved, including the right of reproduction in whole or in part in any form.
SIMON & SCHUSTER BOOKS FOR YOUNG READERS
and related marks are trademarks of Simon & Schuster, Inc.
For information about special discounts for bulk purchases, please contact
Simon & Schuster Special Sales at 1-866-506-1949 or business@simonandschuster.com.
The Simon & Schuster Speakers Bureau can bring authors to your live event.
For more information or to book an event, contact the Simon & Schuster Speakers
Bureau at 1-866-248-3049 or visit our website at www.simonspeakers.com.
The text for this book was set in Goldenbook.
The illustrations for this book were rendered in pencil on paper.
Manufactured in China
0322 SCP
First Edition
2 4 6 8 10 9 7 5 3 1
Library of Congress Cataloging-in-Publication Data
Names: Reynolds, Aaron, 1970– author. | Brown, Peter, 1979– illustrator.
Title: Creepy crayon! / Aaron Reynolds ; illustrated by Peter Brown.
Description: First edition. | New York : Simon & Schuster Books for Young Readers, [2022] | Series:
Creepy tales | Audience: Ages 4-8. | Audience: Grades K-1. | Summary: "When Jasper Rabbit finds
a purple crayon willing to do his schoolwork for him, he is elated—at first"— Provided by publisher.
Identifiers: LCCN 2020034942 (print) | LCCN 2020034943 (ebook) | ISBN 9781534465886
(hardcover) | ISBN 9781534465893 (ebook)
Subjects: CYAC: Rabbits—Fiction. | Crayons—Fiction.
Classification: LCC PZ7.R33213 Crh 2022 (print) | LCC PZ7.R33213 (ebook) | DDC [E]—dc23
LC record available at https://lccn.loc.gov/2020034942
LC ebook record available at https://lccn.loc.gov/2020034943